Toby is invited to go on a picnic with his parents.

E

Toby, Who Are You?

Story by WILLIAM STEIG

Pictures by TERYL EUVREMER

JOANNA COTLER BOOKS

An Imprint of HarperCollinsPublishers

To my wonderful illustrator
—W.S.

To Bill, with love
—T.E.

His father swings Toby up on his shoulders.
"Dad, you're a camel. And I'm your hump,"
says Toby.
"Oh. Is that who I am?" says his father.

Toby's parents think they have found a lovely spot for their picnic, but . . .

"Watch out for that wild bull," yells Toby's mother.

"That wild bull looks familiar," says Toby's father.

"Who is that now, slithering out of your basket?" wonders Toby's father.

"Help!" screams his mother. "I think that's a cobra!"

The creature hisses, spits, and snarls.

Engaged in pleasant chatter, Toby's parents notice a spooky-looking creature hanging from a branch.
"Am I scaring you?" asks Toby.
"No. We like bats," says Toby's father.

Toby loses his grip and falls.

"Now you look a lot like a pig in a puddle,"

says Toby's father.

"Oink," says Toby.

"Where's Toby?" asks his father.

"I don't know," says Toby's mother.

"All I see is that chameleon."

Toby's father whispers in his wife's ear:

"Could that be him?"

"It *is* him!" says Toby. "Can't you see?"

"Tooooby!" his parents call.

"Peck, pick, pack, pock," comes a sound from the trees.

"Is that a peewit up there, do you think?" asks Toby's father.

"NooooO!" says Toby. "Peck, pick, pack, pock . . ."

"Oh," says Toby's father, "you're a woodpecker."

"Whooooo am I now?" asks Toby.

"How can I tell if I can't see you?" exclaims Toby's mother.

"That's a clooooo," says Toby.

"Oh, I get it," says Toby's mother. "It's nighttime and you're an owl!"

"Hey, look! Your hat is walking," says Toby's father.
"That's how Toby imitates a turtle," says Toby's mother.

"It IS a turtle!" cries Toby. "Got you that time."

On the way home, Toby crawls along in the dust.

"Why are you so slow, Toby?" asks his mother.

"Did you ever see a snail in a hurry?" says Toby.

"I'm just about ready for a couple of kisses," cries Toby after his bath.

"We're tigers, and tigers don't give kisses,"
growl Toby's parents.
"Tigers! No you're not . . ." laughs Toby.

"You're kissing bugs, that's who you are!"
Toby allows himself to be kissed.